THE CURSE OF THE CALICO CAT

by **Ellen Weiss** and **Mel Friedman**

illustrated by **Dirk Zimmer**

A STEPPING STONE BOOK

Random House 🏠 **New York**

Library of Congress Cataloging-in-Publication Data
Weiss, Ellen. The curse of the calico cat / by Ellen Weiss and Mel Friedman ; illustrated by Dirk Zimmer. p. cm. "A Stepping stone book."
Summary: Nonnie and her Uncle Paul help her new friends get rid of the evil cat that came along with their ancient family curse.
ISBN 0-679-85405-3 (pbk.) — ISBN 0-679-95405-8 (lib. bdg.)
[1. Cats—Fiction. 2. Blessing and cursing—Fiction.] I. Friedman, Mel. II. Zimmer, Dirk, ill. III. Title.   PZ7.W4475Cu   1994   [Fic]—dc20 93-42552

Manufactured in the United States of America   10 9 8 7 6 5 4 3 2 1

THE CURSE OF THE CALICO CAT

..1

Dear Marissa,

Life has been really stinky since you moved away. Your house is just sitting there empty. There are no decent kids left in the neighborhood. The Terrible Turkel Twins turned three yesterday, and to celebrate, they almost burned down their garage.

I'm so bored and lonely! I miss you so much! Why did you have to move, anyway, you rat?

Well, now that I've got that out of my system, I can go on living. Write back soon.

Love,
Nonnie

Nonnie Kaminsky threw down her pencil and sighed. She folded up the letter and stuffed it into an envelope. Then she grabbed a sweater and ran the two blocks to the mailbox. She wanted to get there before the last pickup of the afternoon.

On the way home from the mailbox she passed the Turkels' house. The twins were in the driveway, bopping each other with toy trains.

When she rounded the corner onto her block, she saw something amazing happening. A moving van had pulled into the driveway of Marissa's house! Four guys with big muscles were attaching a ramp onto the back of the truck. Somebody was really moving in!

Nonnie watched the movers for a few minutes. Then she went home and settled down with her math homework in the big window seat in the living room. She couldn't work, though. Her mind was on the house across the street. Who was moving in there? And did they have any kids?

At last a car pulled up to the big, ramshackle old house. Out popped the new owners: a mother, a father—and, yes! Two kids! And they looked nice! The girl had long black hair halfway down her back. She looked about nine, Nonnie's age.

The boy was dribbling a basketball up to the front door. He looked about seven.

Even though she was dying to go and meet them, Nonnie figured she'd better wait. They were busy.

When her mother walked in the door, Nonnie threw her arms around her. "There's a new family across the street!" she shouted. "And they have kids! And there's a girl my age!"

"Well, hallelujah!" exclaimed her mother.

"Can I go see them tonight, after they're moved in?"

"For a little while, if they don't mind having you. But don't forget, your uncle Paul is coming for dinner."

"Oh, boy!" said Nonnie. Uncle Paul was her favorite relative in the world, next to her mom. He was like a big brother to Nonnie, someone she could always call on for help.

Nonnie spent all afternoon in the big bay window, watching the moving van unload. It was late October. By the time the van finally left it was dark out. Streetlights were blinking on all over the quiet little town of Pequod, Massachusetts.

Then Nonnie saw the lights go on in Marissa's old house. It made her feel funny. She was sad because somebody else was living in her best friend's house. But she was also hopeful that the new girl might be somebody nice.

A little before dinnertime Nonnie heard a strange noise at the front door—a high-pitched yowling sound. It kept going for a while, then stopped. Then there was a scratching on the door.

Nonnie went to the door and opened it a crack. A sudden gust of wind shot a handful of dead leaves through the gap, brushing her ankles. Startled, Nonnie jumped back. Then she looked down.

"Hey, it's just a kitty cat!" she said. She opened the door farther and bent down. "How did you get so dirty?" she asked. The big cat's orange-and-black coat was grimy and matted. Nonnie pulled little bits of leaves from its fur. The cat looked up at her and meowed. Its eyes glowed in the night.

Nonnie's mother came into the hallway, wiping her hands on a dishtowel. "Oh, how sweet," she said. "Where do you think it came from?"

"I don't know," said Nonnie. "I've never seen it before."

"Maybe it belongs to the new people," said her mother. "It could have gotten out while the movers were working."

"I'll go see if it's theirs," said Nonnie. "It'll give me a good reason to visit." She scooped up the cat in her arms and walked across the street. As she rang the doorbell, the cat was purring like an engine. It weighed a ton, thought Nonnie. Her arms were tired already.

After a long wait, the big front door opened slowly. The boy stood there. He looked kind of serious. He had glasses and brown hair that looked like an upside-down bowl.

"Hi," said Nonnie. "I live across the street. My name's Nadja, but I'm called Nonnie. Is this your cat?"

The boy stared at the cat. To Nonnie, his reaction to it seemed bizarre. Could the look on

his face be fear—or even hatred? Nonnie decided she was mistaken. Maybe that was just his normal expression.

"Wh-where did you find it?" he asked.

"It was crying outside our door," replied Nonnie. "Looks like it's been out a while."

The boy lowered his gaze. "I guess we—um—forgot it when we moved," he said. "It must have followed us all the way from Canterbury."

"Are you kidding?" asked Nonnie.

The boy shook his head.

"Wow! That's ten miles from here. You've got some smart cat," said Nonnie. "Well, now it's safe with its family again."

"Uh-huh," the boy said weakly. He took the cat from her but didn't open the door any farther.

Wasn't he going to invite her in? Nonnie wondered.

No. They both just stood there.

"What's the cat's name?" asked Nonnie.

"Tabitha."

"Well, I guess I better be going," Nonnie said finally.

"Yeah. Me too," said the boy. Then he seemed to remember his manners. "My name's Eli White," he said, "and I've got a sister named Jessica."

"Welcome to the neighborhood," said Nonnie.

"Thanks."

"Well, bye."

"Bye," said Eli. "See you around."

"Sure," said Nonnie, shuffling off the porch.

On the way home she couldn't help feeling let down. Eli White didn't seem very friendly at all. He could have invited her in, at least for a minute.

Maybe he acted that way because he was a boy, and younger, Nonnie told herself. Then she had a depressing thought. What if all the Whites were strange? What if Jessica White was as weird as her brother?

Nonnie needed someone to cheer her up. She was really glad that Uncle Paul was coming for dinner.

2

Uncle Paul could hardly focus on Nonnie's worries. He had problems of his own.

"Dunstan Muckthorpe's after me," he said as they ate pizza.

"Who's Dunstan Muckthorpe?" asked Nonnie. She pulled out a long string of cheese from her slice.

"He's this rich old guy who lives across town."

Nonnie's mother came in with the salad. "Muckthorpe..." she said, setting the bowl on the table. "Muckthorpe—isn't he the one who bought the orphanage?" She snapped her fingers. "I remember! He installed pay toilets! The kids had to put in a dime every time they wanted to go to the bathroom."

"That's him," said Uncle Paul. "He rides a

motor scooter because he's too cheap to buy gas for a car."

"Wow! That's cheap," said Nonnie.

"He wants to buy my land, bulldoze the emporium, and put up an apartment building. A big, ugly, high-priced one."

"You're kidding," said Nonnie.

Paul frowned. "Wish I were."

Nonnie was stunned. "Knock down the emporium? He can't do that. Everybody loves your place."

The Used Everything Emporium was famous all over Pequod. It had a little bit of everything: ancient books, strange and useless antique kitchen gadgets, nifty old toys. There was also about an acre of wonderful old cars that Paul let little kids sit in and pretend to drive. "Nothing new under the sun" was the store's motto. It was right above the front gates.

Nonnie knew that Uncle Paul couldn't live for a minute without the emporium. It was his whole life. He would never sell it—especially not to a

guy who wanted to put up a bunch of fancy apartments.

"I don't see what the problem is," Nonnie said. "Just don't sell it to him."

"It's not so easy," Uncle Paul replied. "He's trying to force me out. He's hoping he can make life so unpleasant for me that I'll give in and sell to him."

"How?"

"Well, two weeks ago my electric trains had a mysterious wreck. Last Thursday somebody broke in and stole three cartons of rare comic books. And yesterday a flood in the basement destroyed my priceless collection of Seashell Art from Around the World."

"Oh, no! Not the seashell picture of Elvis Presley!"

"Yup," said Uncle Paul. His six-foot frame slumped down into his chair, and he ran his fingers back through his hair. He always did that when he was upset.

"This is serious," said Nonnie. "We have to

fight back. We can't let this guy win."

"Definitely not," said Uncle Paul. "I'm going to beat him. I don't know how, but I'll find a way."

They talked about Muckthorpe until dessert, when the conversation turned to the Kaminskys' new neighbors.

"I'm sure they just need a little time to adjust," said Nonnie's mother.

"Maybe," said Nonnie. "But he could have invited me in for at least a minute."

"They might have some deep, dark secret in there," Uncle Paul said. "Like a monster on a chain." He raised his arms like a bear and growled.

"No, silly," said Nonnie. "They're regular."

"You could invite the girl over after school sometime," said her mom.

"Well…maybe," said Nonnie.

"It would be great for you to have a friend across the street again," said her mother.

"I know," said Nonnie. "But what kind of people would move away and leave their cat behind?

That boy did not look happy when I brought it back."

"Hmmmmm," said Paul. "This is not a good picture you're painting."

"Stop it, both of you," said Nonnie's mother. "Give them a chance. Maybe things are not what they seem."

3

The next day after school Nonnie rang the door-bell at the Whites' house. It looked as if nobody was home. The shades and blinds were all drawn, and no lights were on.

Just as Nonnie was turning to go, the door opened. But just a crack. The girl was at the door this time.

Nonnie glanced down. The cat sat at the girl's feet, staring up at Nonnie. Somehow it didn't look so friendly today.

"Hi," said Nonnie. "I'm Nonnie Kaminsky."

"I know," said the girl. "Eli told me about you. My name's Jessica." She smiled. She had the sweetest smile Nonnie had ever seen, a smile that

lit up her whole face. But she didn't open the door any farther.

"I thought...maybe we could do something sometime," said Nonnie. "Like you could come over to my house or something."

Jessica's smile grew even wider. "Thanks!" she said. "That would be great!"

Then she froze. A cloud seemed to come over her sunny face. She slipped outside the house and shut the door behind her.

"I'd love to come over," she said so softly she was almost whispering. "It's just that I'm not sure I'm...allowed." She looked nervously over her shoulder, as if someone were watching.

Boy, thought Nonnie, Jessica's parents must be really strict.

She decided to try again. "Well, maybe I could come over to your house sometime—if your parents wouldn't mind. I'm really a nice person and everything. And my mother's a schoolteacher."

Jessica blushed a deep red. "You don't understand. It's not—"

She broke off as a car door slammed in the

driveway. Jessica's mother was home. She came staggering up the walk with two heavy grocery bags.

Jessica ran and took a bag from her mother. "Can I take the other one?" Nonnie asked Mrs. White.

"It's okay," said Jessica's mother. "I'm fine with this one. But thanks for asking." She had the same beautiful smile as Jessica.

Jessica introduced Nonnie to her mother. "It's wonderful to have a nice girl Jessica's age, and right across the street!" said Mrs. White warmly.

Nonnie could see that the bag was very heavy. It sagged in Mrs. White's arms. "Really, I can help you carry that," she offered again.

Jessica's mother gripped the bag tightly. "I'm fine, Nonnie," she said. "Really."

Suddenly the bag broke at the bottom. Its contents spilled out all over the walk.

It had been full of enormous bloody bones.

Nonnie gasped. She saw Jessica and her mother exchange an odd, tense look.

"We're—uh—making soup today," said Mrs. White to Nonnie.

"They're for our cat," said Jessica at exactly the same time.

The two of them looked at each other quickly. "We're making soup for our cat," said Mrs. White.

Suddenly Jessica started scratching her nose as if it were itching unbearably. She gave her mother a desperate look and burst into tears.

"I'm sorry. I can't stay out here anymore," she cried. She pushed past Nonnie, threw open the door, and fled into the house. "I'm sorry," Nonnie heard her sob.

Mrs. White looked upset, too. Her eyes were tearing as she wearily gathered up the bones and piled them onto the broken bag. "Thanks for trying to help, honey," she said. "Please excuse Jessica. She sometimes gets these—uh—bad allergy attacks. I know she'll want to see you again." And then she, too, was gone.

Nonnie walked down the path feeling really

confused. When she was halfway to the street,
she turned to look back at the house.

Through the tangled, dark branches of an oak
tree she could see the Whites' cat sitting in the
front window, licking a paw and watching her.
Maybe it was only a reflection from the streetlights, but the cat's eyes seemed to be glowing.

4

After school the next day Nonnie ran right over to the Used Everything Emporium. She had decided she needed some expert help. But when she got there, her uncle was busy. He was having an argument with an old man outside his front door.

This could have been only one person: Dunstan Muckthorpe. His features were twisted into a frightful scowl.

"I *deserve* to have this land!" he shouted in a cracked voice. His left eye twitched, and his thin white hair stood on end. "And you don't! What do you use it for? Junk! Useless junk! And what am I going to use it for? I'll tell you what! Nice apartments for rich people! Rich people have a hard

time finding places to live that are good enough for them. It's a terrible problem! And you, my friend, are standing in their way! You ought to be ashamed!"

Nonnie could see that Uncle Paul was having trouble controlling himself. "I am going to count to three," he said. "And I want you off my land before I am finished. One."

Muckthorpe began walking backward. "Don't think I can't make you sell!" he barked.

"Two."

"I own every piece of land around yours now. I need yours, and I'm going to get it." Paul took a step toward him and Muckthorpe walked backward a little faster.

"Three!"

Muckthorpe turned around and broke into a run. He jumped onto his motor scooter and buzzed away, shaking his fist behind him.

"Wow! You sure took care of him," said Nonnie.

"He'll be back," said Uncle Paul.

They sat down on the front steps and chewed

on blades of grass. "Sorry you got such a nasty greeting," Paul said. "What brings you here?"

"I think there's something strange going on in the house across the street," said Nonnie.

"The people with the Deep, Dark Secret?" he asked.

She nodded. "And you want to hear something really weird?"

"Naturally."

"I think it has something to do with their cat."

Paul did a double take. "Say what?"

"Tell me if I'm crazy. I think their cat has them scared."

Her uncle chewed for a minute on his piece of grass.

"Follow me," he said. He stood up and led Nonnie inside the emporium.

In a far corner, covered with dust, was a wooden chest. It was full of very old books. Paul opened the lid and started poking inside it. As he did, clouds of yellow dust rose into the air.

"Let's see. I remember getting a book in last month that just might help." He pulled one out.

"*The Butler's Handbook*? No, that's not it. How about *Traveling in Borneo*...? No. Ah, here it is. *Cursed Creatures of Massachusetts*. Written by one Martha Farnsworth, Boston, 1789." He blew some dust off the cover.

"Wow. That's more than two hundred years old," Nonnie said. She bent to read over his shoulder. The print was tiny, and there were lots of strange old ink drawings of animals.

As Uncle Paul flipped through the book, Nonnie saw some amazing chapter titles fly by: The Terrible Terrier of Taunton, The Fearsome Flying Fish of Framingham, and The Moaning Mole of Medford.

"Not so fast," she told him. "This looks really interesting."

The tiny string of bells that hung on the shop door started jangling. "That's the guy who's fixing my back steps," said Paul. "Somebody poured tar all over them last night."

"Oh, how awful!" exclaimed Nonnie. "Do you think it was Muckthorpe?"

"I have no doubt," said Paul grimly.

"Can't you have him arrested or something?"

Paul sighed. "He's too clever. I have no real proof." The bells jangled again. "In the meantime, I've got to fix my steps. Why don't you take this book home with you? Maybe you'll find what you're looking for."

Nonnie said good-bye to her uncle and walked home with the heavy book in her knapsack. She was thinking about that rotten Dunstan Muckthorpe. If only he weren't so slippery!

But when she was almost at her door, her thoughts were suddenly interrupted. Somebody was screaming!

5

Nonnie ran toward the sound. It was coming from inside Jessica's house.

The front door was unlocked. Nonnie ran into the house without even stopping to knock. What on earth could be wrong?

Then she saw Jessica. She was screaming, running up the stairs to the second floor. The cat was right on her heels, puffed out to twice its size. It looked almost as if it were chasing her.

"Jessica!" yelled Nonnie.

Jessica and the cat both whirled around at the same time. The cat stared right at Nonnie in a way that made her afraid. Then it let out a tremendous hiss. It sprang through the air toward Nonnie, missing her face by two inches. It

landed beside her and streaked off toward the kitchen, still hissing.

"Come up to my room," whispered Jessica. "I have to talk to you. Quick, before the cat comes back!"

Nonnie hesitated, and Jessica waved her arm. "Quick! Come! We have to move fast!"

Nonnie sprinted up the stairs.

Jessica headed for the room on the

right of the landing. It was the one that had been Marissa's brother's room. Nonnie glimpsed the cat on the stairs behind them.

They ran into the bedroom and Jessica slammed the door just as the cat reached the landing.

Nonnie looked around, panting. Jessica's room was pretty but very dark.

The two of them sat down on the bed. Then Jessica jumped up. She turned on her portable radio very loud. The traffic report was on.

"Isn't there any music on?" asked Nonnie. The noise was hurting her ears.

Jessica put her finger up to her lips. Then she sat down again on the bed and whispered something to Nonnie.

"What?" said Nonnie. "I can't hear you."

"I'm trying to drown out our voices."

This was very strange.

"I guess you're wondering about our cat," Jessica whispered a little louder.

"Well, yeah, kind of," said Nonnie.

"We have to whisper," said Jessica. "It can hear every little noise."

Underneath the closed door Nonnie could see four dark little feet pacing back and forth.

"It isn't really our cat," Jessica whispered. "At least we don't want it to be. It's part of a curse that's hundreds of years old. This same cat has been in our family for generations." Jessica looked nervously at the door before she continued. "It's not our pet—we're *its* pets."

"Omigod!" Nonnie blurted.

"Shhh!" warned Jessica. "We've tried everything to get rid of it. We've looked in books, we've talked to experts. But we can't make it leave. It always comes back. We even tried locking it in the basement and moving away from Canterbury, but it got out and found us. It makes our lives miserable. And there's no way to destroy it."

"What does it do?"

"All kinds of horrible stuff. We have to do whatever it wants. For one thing, it hates light. We have to keep the curtains closed all the time.

Also, it doesn't like us to leave the house. If it's mad at us, it punishes us. Usually it makes us itch. It's as bad as poison ivy. It starts with your nose, then it spreads. If it's in a bad mood, it scratches us. And sometimes it makes our faces get all scrunched up."

"That's awful!"

"It makes us feed it those big, awful bones. And candy corn. And these mushrooms that only grow in caves in Bulgaria."

"Yuck!"

"It doesn't like us to have visitors. If anybody comes, it tries to scare them away. That's what it was doing to you on the stairs. We don't ever, ever get to have friends." She looked down, twisting the bedspread in her hands.

"I'll be your friend," said Nonnie.

Jessica gave her a hug. She looked as if she were about to cry.

The four feet were pacing faster outside in the hallway. In a moment a thumping began on the door.

"Why was it chasing you up the stairs before?" Nonnie asked.

"I think it might have been revenge. It's mad that we tried to leave it behind when we moved."

"We have to get rid of this cat," whispered Nonnie. "We *will* get rid of it. I'll help you." Nonnie heard a deep moaning growl outside the door.

Jessica suddenly started madly scratching her nose. "Oh, no!" she said. "I'm itching. We'd better stop. It knows."

"Do you think it could hurt me, too?" Nonnie asked.

"I'm not sure, but I don't think so. It's our curse. I haven't seen it actually hurt anybody else, just scare them."

Jessica's upper lip started twisting up toward her right eye. "We'd better go downstairs," she said.

When they opened the door, the cat was nowhere to be seen.

They went downstairs, and Nonnie got her

first good look at the rest of the house. All the familiar rooms looked so different now! Dark curtains covered all the windows, and there were long, deep scratch marks in the wallpaper. The furniture was all clawed to shreds, too.

Nonnie was heartsick. When Marissa lived here, the house was filled with light and pretty furniture and plants. But this—this was so depressing!

While they were standing in the living room, the front door opened. Jessica's parents and Eli came in. They were all carrying heavy grocery bags—more bones, Nonnie figured.

They all looked shocked to see Nonnie in the house.

Jessica mouthed words at them: *She knows.* Nonnie nodded to show them it was true. The cat sat on the coffee table, watching them carefully.

The girls helped carry the bags into the kitchen, and Jessica introduced Nonnie to her dad.

"Well, Nonnie," said Mr. White, "as long as—well, as long as you know—maybe you'd like to stay for dinner. We haven't had anybody to dinner in years."

"Okay," said Nonnie. She glanced nervously at the cat, which was now sitting in the kitchen doorway. "I just have to call my mother and see if it's all right." She was half hoping her mother would say no. She dialed home from the kitchen phone.

"Why, that's lovely, darling," said Nonnie's mother. "Have a good time. And don't forget to say thank you."

"I can stay," said Nonnie after she hung up.

"Just expect things to be a little…weird," said Eli.

"I definitely will," said Nonnie with a shiver.

"Why don't you kids keep yourselves busy till dinner's ready?" said Mr. White. "It'll be about twenty minutes."

The kids went into the den. "So," said Nonnie, "do you have any games?"

"Most of our stuff is still packed," said Jessica. She pointed to a ceiling-high pile of boxes against the wall.

"Why don't we watch TV, then?" Nonnie said. As she said it, she noticed that the cat was sitting on the arm of the sofa, staring at the TV screen.

"We can try," said Eli. He exchanged a look with Jessica. These looks were becoming familiar to Nonnie.

Jessica switched on the set. Then the three of them settled down in front of the television.

"There's supposed to be a good new science show on this afternoon," said Nonnie. "Could we watch that?"

Jessica knitted her brow. "How about *I Love Lucy*?" she said.

"*I Love Lucy*? Give me a break!" said Nonnie. "Haven't you seen every one that was ever made?"

"Yes," said Jessica. "We…watch it a lot." She kept pointing her chin toward the cat. Nonnie didn't catch on right away.

"Why don't we try this other show for a few minutes?" Nonnie asked. "It's on channel 12."

Jessica took a deep breath. "Okay," she said. "We can try it. But I can't promise anything."

As the *Lucy* theme came on, Jessica changed the channel. Suddenly the cat took a flying leap off the arm of the sofa and landed on Jessica's lap.

"Ow!" said Jessica. The cat jumped onto the floor and licked its paw. Nonnie saw a long, bleeding scratch on Jessica's arm.

"Oh, Jessica!" cried Nonnie.

"We have to watch *Lucy*," said Jessica, fighting back tears. "The cat only likes *Lucy*."

Nonnie looked at the cat with hatred. *You selfish creep!* she thought.

They watched *Lucy* in silence until dinnertime. The cat didn't budge. During the commercials it turned its head slightly to fix them with an icy stare.

"Dinner!" called Mr. White.

Dinner looked great: chicken, rice, and salad. "My mom hardly ever has time to cook," Nonnie said to Jessica's parents as they sat down at the kitchen table. "She has to teach and mark papers. And she's going to school, too. Her best dish is canned chicken noodle soup."

Although the food was delicious, the meal was less than cheerful. The cat crouched in the corner, making loud slobbering noises as it gobbled down a bowl of Bulgarian mushrooms. As soon as it finished, it jumped right onto the table and stared coldly at Mr. White.

"Oh, sorry," he said, and hurried off to the refrigerator. When he came back, he was carrying a plate full of huge bones. He set it on the floor near the table, and the cat leaped on it with a roar. Then it proceeded to devour the bones, crunching and slurping and cracking. The din was so loud that no one could talk.

In about five minutes the bones were gone and the cat's face was covered with blood. Nonnie was so disgusted she couldn't finish her chicken. The cat licked its lips.

Nonnie glared at the cat. *Selfish and rude and disgusting!* she thought. *Well, we're going to deal with you, Tabitha.*

"Who's going to do the napkin today?" asked Mrs. White.

"It's my turn," Eli said, sighing. He got up from his chair and walked to the cupboard. Reaching up, he pulled down a frilly lace napkin from a shelf. He walked over to the cat and dabbed its face. The cat sat there like an empress.

"Don't forget the candy corn," said Jessica.

"Oh, right," said Eli. He filled a large bowl with candy corn for the cat. "There you go, Tabitha," he said. "Knock yourself out."

The cat hissed at him, then wolfed down the candy corn.

Nonnie stared at her plate.

"And that," said Mr. White, "is dinner at the White household."

"Thank you very much," said Nonnie politely. "It was very good."

Dear Marissa,
Well, some people moved into your house. Their name is the Whites, and they have two kids. One is even a girl my age. She's nice.

But guess what? There's a <u>curse</u> on them!
I think I'm going to have an adventure. I'm
scared, but I'm excited, too. Wish me luck.

    I miss you. I wish you were still here. Do
you have any new friends yet?

Love,
Nonnie

6

As soon as Nonnie got home, she remembered the book Uncle Paul had given her. *Cursed Creatures of Massachusetts*. Maybe there would be something helpful in it.

She pulled it out of her knapsack and heaved it onto her desk. The book gave off a cloud of dust that made her sneeze.

The table of contents had tiny, old-fashioned writing. Nonnie moved her finger down the list, muttering to herself. "Let's see...Vampire Skunk of Stockbridge...Ghost Possum of Plymouth...Wait a second! The Evil Cat of Cambridge!" She turned to page 79, only to find

that the Evil Cat of Cambridge was a black cat, not a calico. In 1702 it had stolen 4,864 socks from people in Cambridge, Massachusetts, and dropped them all down the town well.

Back to the table of contents. As she kept reading, Nonnie discovered that there were lots and lots of cursed cats, along with a lot of dogs, a few snakes, and at least one cursed chipmunk. It was going to be a long night.

She was still at it at eight thirty, when her mother poked her head into Nonnie's room. "Finished your homework, darling?" she asked. Nonnie gulped. She hadn't even *started* her homework.

"I have a lot tonight," she said. "I might be up for a while."

"Not too late, okay?"

"Okay, Mom."

"How was your dinner across the street?"

"It was very interesting."

"That's good."

A few minutes later Nonnie came to a

chapter called The Curse of the Calico Cat. She read:

There lived in the Town of Canterbury, in the Colony of Massachusetts, a very evil Witch. And it came to pass that this Witch, being Discovered, was driven from the Town in the Year of Our Lord 1693. But before she took her leave, she swore an Oath of Vengeance. Her Calico Cat was to be the means of her Revenge. From that time forth, this Cat was to be a Curse upon whatever Persons gave it shelter. The Cat would pass down the Generations of the Family, and only die when the last Member of the Family passed away.

There is only one way to be rid of the Curse of the Calico Cat. The Cat must be Transferred to another Person. This is done by means of a Ceremony, which must be performed in a Graveyard at Midnight on All Hallows' Eve.

These Words must be said by the accursed Person:

Birds of the Air,
Fish of the Sea,
Beasts of the Land,
From this Cat make me free!

This Person must be holding a Part of each Creature named in the Chant. It may be a Feather, a Scale, a Hoof, or any other Part.

In addition, the Person who shall receive the Cat must be made to say these Words:

Birds of the Air,
Fish of the Sea,
Beasts of the Land,
Let this Cat come to me!

Only in such a way can an unfortunate Person be rid of the Curse of the Calico Cat.

Wow! This was amazing! Nonnie had really found it—the Curse of the Calico Cat! It had to be Jessica's cat. It was calico, it came from Canterbury, and it was definitely a curse.

Nonnie closed the book. All she had to do now was follow the directions and get rid of the cat. Then she'd have a new friend who lived in a normal house, and they wouldn't ever have to watch *Lucy* reruns again.

Nonnie rushed through her homework and got into bed. But she was too excited to go to sleep. And when she did finally fall asleep, her sleep was fitful and restless.

The next thing she knew she was sitting bolt

upright, drenched in sweat. Her heart was pounding. She had dreamed that the cat had been sitting at the foot of her bed, staring at her. She could feel its terrible thoughts: *You will never defeat me!*

She reached over and picked up her clock. Four thirty-five.

It was only a dream, she told herself. Only a dream. But it had seemed so *real*.

7

The next day Nonnie jumped on her bike after school and pedaled as fast as she could to the Used Everything Emporium.

"Uncle Paul!" she yelled as she put down the kickstand. "Uncle Paul! I figured it out! It's the Calico Cat!"

Paul came out, wiping some grease off his hands. "What's the Calico Cat?"

"The cat across the street! It's a curse! There's only one way to get rid of it. In a grave-yard at midnight on Halloween!"

"Whoa, whoa, whoa. Could we go a little slower here?"

So Nonnie sat down with her uncle on the

fender of an old Chevy and explained the whole thing from the beginning. She told him about the witch and the curse and the chant.

"I'm going to get Jessica and Eli," she said. "And we'll go to a graveyard. Halloween's only three days away—isn't that lucky? And we'll get, like, maybe a bird feather and a couple of shrimps from the fish store and a leather shoe or something, and we'll go there at midnight and do the ceremony. What do you think?"

"I think it's a great idea. You sure don't have much to lose, except a little sleep. But there are just a few problems, Nonnie."

"What are they?"

"One: There isn't a graveyard within thirty miles of here. Two: Your mom wouldn't let you visit a graveyard at midnight even if there *was* one. Three: Who are you going to transfer the cat to? And how are you going to get this person to say such a ridiculous poem? That is, *if* this whole thing isn't some made-up piece of silliness about a perfectly normal cat. Maybe a very grouchy cat, but a normal cat."

"Hmmm," said Nonnie. "I'm positive this is the right cat. But I'll have to think about the other problems."

"Okay. I'll think about them, too."

On the way home Nonnie stopped at Jessica's house and rang the bell. When Jessica answered the door, Nonnie put her finger to her lips. "Shhh," she said.

The cat was sitting in the living room doorway watching them. It looked just like anybody else's pet cat—unless you *knew*. Nonnie thought she saw an evil gleam in its eyes. Would it try to hurt her?

Nonnie dug around the candy wrappers and balled-up old math homework in her knapsack until she came up with a pencil and some paper. COME TO MY HOUSE, she wrote, and shoved the paper under Jessica's nose.

Without a word, Jessica ran to get her jacket. The girls didn't talk until they were in Nonnie's room with the door shut. Just to be sure, Nonnie put on some loud music.

"I figured it out," Nonnie whispered.

"About the cat?" asked Jessica quietly.

"Yup." Nonnie grinned. She pulled out the old book and showed Jessica the part about the Calico Cat.

"Wow!" said Jessica. "Can we really try the ceremony?"

"If we can get permission to go out in the middle of the night, sneak past the cat, go to a cemetery, find someone to transfer the cat to, and make them say the words. No problem."

"Maybe your uncle Paul could help us figure something out. Could we say we're spending the night at his place? There's a funny idea— Halloween at a junk store and auto graveyard."

"It's not junk," Nonnie started to reply, but then she stopped short. "Wait a second—auto graveyard. Graveyard! Cemetery! The book didn't say what *kind* of graveyard you have to do it in. Maybe an auto graveyard would work."

"It's a really weird idea—"

"But—"

"But it might work!" shouted Jessica.

"Shhh!" said Nonnie.

"Okay," said Jessica, quieting down. "Now, who can we give the cat to?"

"You think about it while I call up my uncle and see if we can do it at his place."

Nonnie went into her mother's bedroom to call Uncle Paul.

"Hello!" he snapped.

"Hi, Uncle Paul. I just wanted to—"

"I'm a little busy now, Nonnie," he interrupted. "There are about a thousand cockroaches in my store. That rotten Muckthorpe!"

In a flash Nonnie had the key to the whole situation. "Can I just ask you one fast question?" she asked her uncle. "Could we—Jessica and Eli and I—come over to your place on Halloween night?"

"What about the curse? And all your big plans?"

"Everything's working out fine. I'll tell you about it later."

"Fine," said Paul. "I gotta go now."

"Okay, thanks—bye!" said Nonnie. "Sorry about your bugs."

"Yeah, me too. Bye."

Nonnie raced back to her bedroom. "We can use Uncle Paul's place!" she crowed. "And guess what? I know just the person who deserves the cat!"

But Jessica didn't seem to hear Nonnie. She was staring out the window. She looked terrified.

Then Nonnie saw why. Right outside the window, *the second-floor window*, was the cat. It seemed to be standing on air, and it was looking into Nonnie's room. Its eyes burned in the twilight.

Nonnie fought the urge to scream. She walked quickly over to the window. Grabbing the curtains, she whipped them closed.

"This means war," she said.

8

The next two days were very busy.

First there was the matter of getting permission to spend Halloween night at Uncle Paul's.

"Do you think your parents will let you have a sleepover there?" Nonnie asked Jessica. They were in the park, kicking through a pile of leaves. It was a good place to talk, far from the cat's ears.

"They'll probably say yes. They feel so bad for us because the cat doesn't let us have any friends. They'll just be glad we got invited somewhere."

"Yeah." Nonnie giggled. "To a graveyard."

The second problem was the list of things they had to collect for the ceremony. "Let's see," said Nonnie. "Birds, fish, and beasts."

"I can bring a can of tunafish," said Jessica.

"Good. That's fish. For beasts, I could bring this deer's jawbone I found in the woods."

"Great. Now, what can we do for a bird?" Jessica wondered. "I don't think I have any bird stuff around. Do you?"

"No, I don't think—hey, wait a second, what's this?" Nonnie bent down and picked something up off the ground. "A blue jay feather!"

"It's a sign! Don't you think so?"

"Definitely," agreed Nonnie.

The girls grinned at each other, and Nonnie carefully put the feather into her pocket.

"Now for problem number three," said Nonnie. "The hard part. Transferring the cat to Mr. Dunstan Muckthorpe."

"Who's that?" asked Jessica.

Nonnie told her all about Muckthorpe and what he'd been doing to Uncle Paul.

"Oh, he and that cat were made for each other!" Jessica exclaimed. "He should *have* that cat!"

"Now, the question is, how are we going to

get him to Uncle Paul's at midnight?"

"And how are we going to get him to say the words?" added Jessica.

"Let's go over to the Used Everything Emporium," said Nonnie. "Maybe Uncle Paul will have some ideas."

They found Paul sitting on the front steps of the emporium. Nonnie introduced him to Jessica.

"Nice to meet you, Jessica," said Paul. "I've heard a lot about you—and your cat."

"Uncle Paul," said Nonnie, "why are you sitting out here? It's cold."

"Can't go inside," he explained. "Roach spray. Had to have the place fumigated. Smells awful."

"Yuck," said Nonnie.

They sat down on the steps, and Nonnie explained the whole plan for the ceremony to her uncle.

"I can't say I believe any of this," said Paul. "But it will be fun anyhow. I'd love to give Muckthorpe a little taste of his own medicine."

"We've solved all the problems but one," said

Nonnie. "How to transfer the cat to Dunstan Muckthorpe. Got any ideas?"

Paul stood up. "Wait here a minute," he said. "I'm having a brainstorm."

He went into the store. A minute later he came out with a lined yellow pad and a green pen that said WORLD'S FAIR 1964 on it. He began writing.

In a few minutes he handed this note to Nonnie:

TO: *Dunstan Muckthorpe*
FROM: *Paul Brent*
I am willing to talk to you about selling my land. Come at twelve midnight on October 31. Alone. No lawyers.

"Wow!" said Nonnie. "Brilliant! Do you think he'll come?"

"He wants this place so badly he'll do anything to get it. He'll come."

"How are we going to get him to say the words?"

"Leave it to me. I'll have it figured out before Halloween."

Nonnie jumped up and threw her arms around her uncle. "Thank you!" she cried. "This is going to work! I know it is!"

"It's pretty darned silly," he said with a grin. "But what the heck."

"Thank you so much for helping us!" Jessica said to him. "You don't know how awful it is being a slave to that cat!"

"No problem," said Uncle Paul. "We're going to have a very unusual Halloween."

That evening after supper Nonnie stood in the kitchen with her mother. She rinsed the plates, and her mother loaded them into the dishwasher.

"So can I go and have a sleepover at Uncle Paul's with Jessica and Eli on Halloween?" she said. "You *have* to say yes. It's important."

"I wish I knew what the big deal was about your going over there. What are you doing that's so important, anyhow?"

"Can I tell you when it's all over, Mom? It'll take me an hour to explain, and I gotta go make plans with Jessica."

"It seems like she's really becoming a friend."

"I guess she is," said Nonnie, taking off her apron. "But everything will be easier when we get rid of the cat." She gave her mother a fast kiss.

"Get rid of the cat?" repeated her mother.

But Nonnie was already out the door.

9

And then at last it was Friday—Halloween.

The wind whipped at the bare trees. In the late afternoon a cold drizzle began to fall. The sky was as gray as stone. A few shivering trick-or-treaters came to Nonnie's door, but they looked eager to get home. Nonnie realized that she hadn't even thought of trick-or-treating—she had more important Halloween things to do.

It seemed to get dark even earlier than usual. By five thirty, the streetlights had come on. Nonnie looked out her front window, wishing it were time to go to Paul's and start the ceremony. The cat was sitting in Jessica's front window,

staring straight at Nonnie. Its eyes were glowing even more brightly than usual. They looked like red coals. Nonnie closed the blinds fast. "Your time is up, cat," she muttered grimly. "So long."

At eight o'clock Nonnie went across the street to pick up Jessica and Eli. They were waiting for her.

"The cat's having a nap," whispered Eli. "It's a good time to sneak out."

Mrs. White came downstairs. "Do you all have your sleeping bags?" she asked.

"Got everything," said Eli.

"Are you planning to bob for apples?" Mrs. White asked, straightening Jessica's jacket for her.

"I—I don't think so," said Nonnie. "We have some other things planned."

Jessica eyed the cat nervously. "Gotta go, Mom," she said.

Mrs. White ran into the kitchen and appeared again with a bag of apples. "It's not a real Halloween party unless you bob for apples," she said.

"Thanks, Mom," said Jessica. She took the

bag and kissed her mother quickly. "See you in the morning."

Jessica, Nonnie, and Eli walked down the driveway, waiting to see if anything was going to happen. So far everything was quiet.

"Jessica, do you have the box with the feather and everything?" Nonnie asked. They had put all the things for the ceremony into a Tupperware container.

"Got it," said Jessica. "Right in my overnight bag."

About three blocks into the walk Jessica started sneezing. She sneezed and sneezed.

"Tabitha must have woken up," said Eli. He walked quickly, determined not to sneeze. But Nonnie could see his face twisting up into a funny shape. Even Nonnie felt her nose itching.

By the time they got to Uncle Paul's place Jessica had finally stopped sneezing, and Eli's face had calmed down. Maybe they were out of the cat's range, thought Nonnie.

The shop was warm and cozy on this chilly

night. Paul had put out cookies and soda for them. "I thought I'd make it at least a little like a party," he said.

"Thanks, Uncle Paul," said Nonnie. "I'm feeling too nervous to have any fun, though."

"Me too," said Jessica.

"Well, what are we going to do for the next three hours?" asked Eli. "It's only eight thirty."

"Why don't we bob for apples?" joked Jessica.

"Hey! That's a good idea," said Uncle Paul. "Did you ever do it? It's really fun."

The three kids looked at one another. "Well, why not?" said Eli. "We have nothing else to do. We told our parents we were coming for a party. We might as well have a party."

Paul brought out a big old copper tub and filled it with water, and they all bobbed for apples. It turned out to be fun, in a drippy way.

When they were done, they ate the apples and the cookies and told all the worst jokes they could think of.

"Do you want to tell scary stories?" Nonnie asked.

"Scary stories don't do much for me," said Jessica, turning serious. "We have a real-life curse right in our house. That's worse than any story."

"Speaking of which," said Uncle Paul, "I think it's time to set things up. Where do you think we should do our cat-transfer ceremony?"

"How about if we do it in the front yard, right outside the door?" said Nonnie.

They went out and took a look. "I guess it's as good a place as any," said Paul.

"Maybe we should draw a circle on the ground to put all of the stuff in," said Eli. "I mean, the bird, beast, and fish stuff."

"Why not?" said Nonnie. "Jessica, let's get out all the things."

"Okay," said Jessica. She unzipped her overnight bag and took out the plastic container.

She opened the lid and gasped.

"What's the matter?" asked Nonnie.

"Look!"

Jessica put her hand into the container and

came out with a handful of…dust. The wind blew
it out of her hand.

"Oh, no!" wailed Nonnie.

"The cat!" said Eli. "The cat did this."

"Okay. Let's deal with it. Can we get together
new things for the spell?" said Jessica.

Paul looked at his watch. "No way," he said.
"It's four minutes to twelve. We can't use what's
in my kitchen. I'm a vegetarian. The most we'll
find is leather shoes."

Jessica plopped herself down on the hood of one of the old cars in the yard. "Oh, no, oh, no, oh, no," she moaned. "Don't tell me we're going to have the cat and its stupid bones until next Halloween! I can't wait another whole year!"

Nonnie plopped down next to her. "How could we come so close and not do it?" she said. "We have to finish it! We just have to!" She smacked her hand down on the pink hood of the car.

"Ow!" she yelped.

"What happened?" asked Jessica.

"I hit my hand on something sharp." Nonnie looked to see what had hurt her. "It's a little horse, rearing up," she said. "Oh, I get it. It's a mustang, because the car's a Mustang—" A look began to creep over her face.

"What?" asked Uncle Paul.

"A mustang is a beast of the land!" said Nonnie. "The book just says it has to be a part of a beast of the land, right? It doesn't say it has to be a real *live* beast." She started wiggling the statue off the car. It was rusty, so it wiggled a lot.

"Hey, wait a second," Paul began, but Nonnie kept wiggling.

"Please, oh, please, oh, please," she begged. "This is life or death! We can get it back on somehow."

"Oh, all right," said Paul. He could never say no to Nonnie.

"What other kinds of cars do you have around here?" Nonnie asked him as she wiggled.

"Well, let's see.... What do we still need?"

"A beast of the air and a beast of the sea."

"Hmmm. I have a Barracuda. That's a beast of the sea. It's over there."

He pointed out a red car nearby. Jessica ran over to it. "What could I get off it fast?" she shouted.

"I don't know—maybe a hubcap," answered Paul. He pulled a big screwdriver out of his back pocket and tossed it to her.

"Hey, look at this white one!" yelled Eli from across the yard. "It's a Thunderbird! A beast of the air!"

"Great!" shouted Nonnie. "Rip a piece off it quick!"

Uncle Paul winced. "That's a classic car," he groaned.

"I'll be careful," promised Eli. He started jiggling things. "Look, the taillight comes right off," he said happily.

"I've got the hubcap off," said Jessica.

"What time is it?" Eli yelled.

"One minute to midnight!" said Nonnie.

The three of them ran to a clearing in the yard. Jessica used the screwdriver to draw a big circle in the packed dirt. She placed the hubcap in the center of the circle. Eli put in the taillight, and Nonnie put in the mustang statue.

"Okay," said Nonnie. "Ten seconds to go."

Jessica and Eli knelt over the circle. Without a word they joined hands across it.

"Seven seconds."

"Where's Muckthorpe?" muttered Uncle Paul nervously.

"I hope this works," whispered Jessica. "An auto graveyard and parts from cars."

"Okay, go."

Jessica and Eli squeezed each other's hands tightly and shut their eyes. *"Birds of the air,"* they recited, *"fish of the sea—"*

A motor scooter buzzed to a stop outside the front gate. *"Beasts of the land, from this cat make me free!"*

There. That part was done.

Dunstan Muckthorpe came walking into the yard.

"So, Brent," he said. "You've decided to sell me your land after all. A wise choice. A wise choice." He laughed a crackly laugh.

Without a word Uncle Paul handed him a piece of paper with a lot of writing on it.

"What's this?"

"Our agreement. Read it."

Muckthorpe began reading it to himself.

"No," said Paul. "Read it out loud."

"I don't like to read out loud," said Muckthorpe. "And I don't do what I don't like to do."

"If you don't read it out loud, we don't talk," said Paul.

"All right," said Muckthorpe. "See what a nice fellow I am?" He laughed again, cleared his throat, and began reading.

"'Paul Brent hereby agrees to sell Dunstan Muckthorpe his property, upon which stands the Used Everything Emporium.'"

Nonnie's eyes widened. "You can't do that!" she whispered into Uncle Paul's ear.

"Don't worry," Paul whispered back. "Just listen to every word."

"'Dunstan Muckthorpe will be sole owner of the property and everything on it,'" continued the old man. "'This includes all birds of the air, fish of the sea, and beasts of the land.'"

He looked at Paul. "Strangest document I've ever seen," he said suspiciously.

"My lawyer told me to put it in," said Paul

innocently. "You know, legal language."

"Hrrrmph," growled Muckthorpe. "Lawyers." He continued. "'Let this agreement also include any dog or cat on the property, which, after payment, will come to me, Dunstan Muckthorpe.'"

A tremendous flash of lightning split the sky. It was followed by a loud clap of thunder.

"That's it!" whispered Uncle Paul. "He said all the words!"

The air all around them seemed to crackle, as though it were filled with static. The wind whipped the dust in the yard around. The clouds raced across the sky. And then, suddenly, with an outraged yowl, the cat seemed to drop right out of the sky and land at Muckthorpe's feet.

"Mr. Muckthorpe, meet Tabitha," said Uncle Paul.

Dunstan Muckthorpe was not interested in the cat. It rubbed against his legs, and he pushed it roughly away with his foot. "Get lost," he said. "I hate cats."

"I wouldn't make Tabitha mad if I were you," said Paul.

Muckthorpe was still reading the contract. He scowled. "Weird contract. But you've got yourself a deal, Brent. Let's sign it before it starts raining."

"Hold on a second," said Paul. "You didn't read the rest."

"The rest?"

"On the other side."

Muckthorpe turned the page over and read the last sentence. "'Selling price of the above property is four million dollars. Price is final.'" He began to splutter. "What is this, Brent? Some kind of a joke?"

"Well, actually, it is a sort of a joke," said Paul. "You might not like the punch line, though."

Large raindrops began falling from the sky. "I'll see you in court for this!" Muckthorpe shouted. He turned to leave. "You think you've had problems here? You haven't seen anything yet! Cockroaches are nothing!"

"I'm shaking in my boots," Paul called after Muckthorpe.

The cat was right on Muckthorpe's heels. It jumped onto his shoulders as he kick-started his motor scooter.

"Get off me!" he shouted. He reached up with one hand to remove the cat. But the cat was going nowhere. It dug its claws in. Muckthorpe yowled in pain, batting at the cat.

He drove off in the rain, his scooter weaving crazily down the road.

There was another flash of lightning, which lit up the scooter as it screeched around the corner and out of sight. Muckthorpe was still trying to get the cat off him. And he was sneezing.

"Whew!" said Nonnie. "That was intense!"

"Anyone for doughnuts before bed?" asked Uncle Paul.

10

In the months that followed, Nonnie and Jessica took long bike rides together. One of their favorite things to do was to ride over to Dunstan Muckthorpe's big house and look in the windows. He was always there, walking from room to room, sneezing and sneezing and sneezing. The cat followed, hissing at him.

One day in April, Nonnie went to the supermarket with her mother. She dashed down aisle six to get some Fig Newtons and ran smack into Dunstan Muckthorpe.

"Watch where you're going, you little brat!" he snarled. Nonnie realized that he didn't recognize her. Then he turned away and went back to what he was doing—filling his cart with bags of candy corn.

Nonnie continued down the aisle, smiling and humming the *I Love Lucy* theme song.

Months went by. Muckthorpe was so busy sneezing and waiting on the cat, he didn't bother Uncle Paul anymore.

Over at Jessica and Eli's house, things were a lot different now. The Whites had thrown open all the curtains and blinds and bought all new furniture. They were so happy they planted flowers all over the front lawn.

And one day, when they were really sure the cat was gone for good, the Whites went out and adopted a puppy.

Dear Marissa,

Well, the excitement has died down now. Things are a lot nicer in your old house since we got rid of the curse. I was happy to get your letter, and I'm glad you're making some good friends. I've made a good friend, too.

I still miss you a lot, though.

Love,
Nonnie

About the Authors

ELLEN WEISS and MEL FRIEDMAN are a husband-and-wife team who have written many popular books for young readers, including *The Adventures of Ratman*, *The Tiny Parents*, and *The Poof Point*.

They live in New York with their daughter, Nora, their boxer, Gracie, and no cats.

About the Illustrator

"I have a calico cat named Katze," says DIRK ZIMMER. "And sometimes I'm not sure if I own him or if *he* owns *me*." Dirk Zimmer has illustrated many books, including *The Curse of the Squirrel*, by Laurence Yep, and *The Adventures of Ratman*, by Ellen Weiss and Mel Friedman, both Stepping Stones. He lives in Kingston, New York.